NADEERA GOONETILLEKE

The Secret SWITCH AWAKENING

UNVEILING THE TRUTH BEHIND THE SWITCH

The Secret Switch Awakening

Nadeera Goonetilleke

Published by Nadeera Goonetilleke, 2024.

Copyright Page

Title: *The Secret Switch Awakening*

Subtitle: *Unveiling the Truth behind the Switch*

Author: Nadeera Goonetilleke

THE SECRET SWITCH AWAKENING

First edition. December 22, 2024.

ISBN: 979-8230829256

Written by Nadeera Goonetilleke.

› Chapter 6:

The Unexpected Reunion

› Chapter 7:

A Day of New Beginnings

› Chapter 8:

The Ties That Bind

› Chapter 9:

Homecoming of Hearts

› Final Thoughts:

A Letter to readers on Love and Marriage

Chapter 1:

Boutique Buzz and Biker Blunders

The weekend buzz of Willowdale filled the air as Veronica and her friend Ridma strolled through its lively streets. The pair made an interesting contrast - Ridma, quiet and composed, balanced Veronica's vivacious personality and striking beauty. Both worked in Accounts at Nexus Innovations, and this Saturday seemed perfect for some carefree shopping and friendly chatter.

Their peaceful afternoon took an unexpected turn near a fashionable dress boutique. A motorcycle's roar shattered the calm, and before anyone could react, it grazed Veronica's back. She stumbled, her handbag flying as she fought to keep her balance.

"Oi!" Veronica whirled around, her eyes flashing with anger. "What's the matter with you? Who gave you a license?"

Even the usually reserved Ridma found her voice. "Are you blind?"

The culprits turned out to be two handsome young men who looked like they'd just been caught stealing cookies from a jar. The driver, sporting disheveled black hair beneath his helmet, stumbled over his words despite his deep, charming voice. "Oh wow! I-I'm so sorry, Miss! Truly!"

His friend, wearing flashy sunglasses, quickly echoed the sentiment with an awkward grin.

Veronica wasn't having any of it. "Sorry?" she scoffed, her voice rising. "I could've ended up with a broken leg! Is that worth just a casual 'sorry'?"

The driver, Vihan, raised his hands defensively, but couldn't help sneaking admiring glances at the fiery beauty before him. His friend Kavish noticed too, whispering, "Dude, she's scary but... she's something else."

As the tension crackled between them, Kavish spotted Veronica's fallen handbag. While retrieving it, he noticed a small leather-bound diary slip out. In a split-second decision that would change everything, he quietly pocketed it.

Kavish quickly held out the handbag toward Veronica, his voice oozing with over-the-top politeness. "So sorry, miss. Here's your handbag. We didn't mean to trouble you." He added an innocent grin for good measure, the kind that might have disarmed anyone else—but Veronica was having none of it. Without even a hint of a courteous smile, Veronica grabbed the bag from his hands, her eyes narrowing with irritation. "Next time, watch where you're going," she snapped, her tone cold and commanding. She shot a sharp look at both of them before turning on her heel and striding off toward the boutique, Ridma hastily following behind.

Vihan couldn't help but watch her retreating figure, an amused smile tugging at his lips. Her fiery attitude was equal parts maddening and magnetic. "She's like a firecracker," he muttered under his breath, his voice carrying a hint of wonder. "Fiery, unpredictable, and absolutely impossible to handle... but for some reason, you can't look away."

Kavish let out a soft chuckle, giving Vihan a light nudge. "Careful, mate. Firecrackers are mesmerizing, but they burn hot—and they leave scars."

Vihan smirked, his gaze still fixed on Veronica's determined stride. "Some scars," he replied with a small shrug, "are definitely worth it."

That's when Kavish reached into his pocket and retrieved a small diary with a sleek black cover.

"Guess what I found," he said, a mischievous glint in his eye. The diary bore the name *Veronica Johnson* etched neatly on the cover.

Vihan's expression shifted as an idea sparked to life. "This," he said, holding up the diary with a growing grin, "is our ticket for a second meeting."

The two exchanged a conspiratorial glance, already formulating their plan. They'd follow the girls to find out where they lived, then return the diary later under the guise of an innocent gesture—an opportunity to break the ice and, perhaps, unravel the mystery behind Veronica's fiery charm.

As they revved up the bike to follow the unsuspecting women, Vihan's pulse quickened—not from the thrill of the ride, but from something deeper, more electric. What had started as a fleeting encounter was already tugging at the edges of his carefully ordered life.

The golden afternoon sun lit their path as they trailed at a cautious distance, Kavish's playful jab about "hot chili turning into a firestorm" still echoing in his mind. Neither of them could have imagined that this impulsive chase was about to ignite a chain of events that would change everything.

Chapter 2:

A Salty Encounter

On a bright morning filled with birdsong, two nervous young men found themselves parked outside a cozy house, their motorcycle's engine sputtering into silence. In the garden, a middle-aged woman swept gravel with practiced strokes, pausing only when she noticed the fidgeting visitors at her gate.

"Good morning," she offered warmly. "Can I help you?"

Vihan's voice cracked like a schoolboy's as he asked, "Aunty, is Veronica here?" The question earned him a sharp look from Kavish.

The woman's smile wavered slightly as she studied them. "Yes... and who might you be?"

"We're her friends, Aunty," Kavish jumped in with his most winning smile – the same one he'd perfected during his school days when he'd forgotten his homework.

Inside the house, Veronica and Ridma were busy whisking away at a bowl of chocolate pudding when they heard a voice ring out from the living room.

“Veronica! Two of your friends are here to see you. They’re probably from your office!” Veronica’s mom called out.

Veronica stopped mid-whisk, exchanging puzzled looks with Ridma. "Friends? Nobody from the office knows where I live."

Their curiosity led them to peek around the corner like amateur detectives, only to discover yesterday's motorcycle troublemakers chatting politely with Veronica's father.

"Those rascals actually tracked us down!" Veronica whispered furiously, while Ridma stood in disbelief beside her.

Forced to maintain decorum under her father's watchful eye, Veronica masked her irritation with politeness. When her father suggested serving tea, however, a deliciously wicked idea took shape in her mind.

Back in the kitchen, Veronica slammed the pantry door with barely contained anger. "Can you believe their nerve, Ridma? They must have followed us yesterday!"

"And now they're sitting there like perfect gentlemen," Ridma observed, shaking her head.

A mischievous glint appeared in Veronica's eyes as she reached for the salt container. "Let's see how they handle my 'special' tea blend."

Despite Ridma's hesitation about potential consequences, Veronica proceeded with her prank, measuring out generous spoonfuls of salt instead of sugar. She stirred each cup with exaggerated care, carrying the tray out with an innocent smile that would have made angels jealous.

The results were instantaneous and satisfying. Vihan struggled to maintain his composure, while Kavish nearly choked on his first sip, though both valiantly attempted to compliment the "unique" brew.

Once Veronica's father left the veranda, she dropped all pretense. "Why are you really here?"

The atmosphere shifted as Vihan produced her diary from his pocket. "We found this yesterday after you left and thought you might need it back."

The revelation melted Veronica's anger, replacing it with unexpected guilt. She hadn't even noticed it was missing. "Oh... thank you," she managed, her voice softening.

When pressed about knowing her address, Vihan admitted to following them home, scratching his head sheepishly. "We didn't know how else to find you!"

As the afternoon wore on, something unexpected happened. The initial tension began to dissolve, replaced by genuine laughter and easy conversation. Vihan's natural charm and Kavish's quick wit gradually wore down the girls' defenses, transforming what had started as a confrontation into something altogether different.

By the time the boys left, the salty tea was forgotten, replaced by warm smiles and lighter hearts. In the space of an afternoon, four strangers had somehow begun writing the first chapter of what promised to be an interesting story – whether of friendship or something more, only time would tell.

The sun was setting as Vihan and Kavish rode away, leaving behind a veranda filled with lingering laughter and the subtle promise of new beginnings. Sometimes, it seems, the most unlikely encounters can lead to the most meaningful connections.

Chapter 3:

The Unlikely Coffee Date

The quiet hum of office work was interrupted by the buzz of Veronica's intercom. Expecting a call from the bank, she answered quickly, thinking it was the same guy. "Hello?" she said.

"Hey, Veronica! It's Vihan."

"Vihan? How did you get my office number?"

His laugh echoed through the line, warm and full of mischief. "From your diary," he replied playfully, clearly enjoying himself. Veronica felt a wave of surprise, annoyance, and a strange, unidentifiable emotion all at once.

"At this hour?" she asked, her voice laced with sarcasm. "Is there something more to say about any misplaced items in my bag?" She tried to hold onto her smile, though it wavered as she absentmindedly fidgeted with her pen.

"This is our lunch break, and I assumed you had one too," he responded smoothly. "Thought it might be a good time to call."

The conversation danced between them, playful and light, until Vihan finally reached his point. "I was wondering... if you'd like to grab a coffee after work. If you're free, that is."

Veronica's mind raced ahead of her words. She found herself wanting to say yes but needing a buffer. "Hmm... I'll need to bring Ridma along. She's my tag-along partner, you know?"

"Doesn't matter," Vihan countered without missing a beat. "Kavish is coming too. He'll keep her company while we talk."

Later that evening, the cozy coffee shop embraced them with the warm, inviting scent of freshly ground coffee beans and the soft hum of low conversations filling the air. The dim lighting and rustic décor added to the calm, intimate atmosphere. Veronica and Ridma were the first to arrive, settling into a quiet corner table that overlooked the bustling street outside. Veronica's fingers tapped restlessly against the smooth wooden surface, her mind racing with thoughts. She kept glancing at the door, waiting for the others to arrive, her nerves getting the best of her as she tried to steady herself.

When Vihan and Kavish walked in, she noticed how different they looked in casual clothes – more relaxed, more approachable. Vihan's confident stride and warm smile made her stomach do a little flip she hadn't expected. Kavish followed, his easy-going nature already evident in his relaxed posture and playful grin.

The conversation flowed as naturally as the coffee, weaving between workplace stories and personal anecdotes. Ridma, usually reserved, found herself drawn into animated discussions with Kavish, their shared humor creating its own little bubble of laughter and stolen glances.

"So, Veronica," Vihan leaned forward, his eyes twinkling with mischief, "what happened to that firecracker who nearly took our heads off that first day?"

She met his gaze with a challenging smile. "Oh, she's still here. Just waiting for the right moment to strike."

"Is that a threat or a promise?" he countered, making everyone laugh.

As the evening progressed, the initial awkwardness melted away like sugar in their coffee cups. They discovered shared interests, debated favorite movies, and traded stories about their worst work experiences. Vihan's charm worked its way past Veronica's carefully constructed walls, while Kavish and Ridma seemed to gravitate toward each other naturally, their quiet chemistry obvious to everyone at the table.

The coffee shop's warm lighting cast a gentle glow over their table, creating an intimate atmosphere that made time seem to stand still. Their laughter mingled with the soft background music, and for a few hours, the world outside ceased to exist.

When they finally decided to call it a night, there was an undeniable reluctance in their goodbyes, a quiet tension that hadn't been there before. Veronica found herself lingering at the door, her gaze meeting Vihan's one last time. A smile passed between them, a subtle but meaningful exchange. The evening had shifted something between them, turning what had started as cautious acquaintances into something more—something charged with a new sense of possibility, unspoken but understood.

As she and Ridma walked home, their conversation was filled with excited whispers and knowing looks. "I saw how you were looking at Kavish," Veronica teased, nudging her friend playfully.

Ridma blushed but didn't deny it. "And what about you and Vihan? I've never seen you so... relaxed around someone."

Veronica couldn't argue. Something had shifted during that evening. What had started as a chance encounter with two reckless bikers had evolved into an unexpected connection that left her both excited and nervous about what might come next?

As she lay in bed that night, replaying moments from the evening in her mind, Veronica realized that sometimes the best things in life come from the most unlikely beginnings. A near-accident, a stolen diary, and a salty cup of tea had somehow led to an evening that felt like the start of something special.

Chapter 4:

Double Blessings, Single Path

On a tranquil Saturday evening, Veronica and Ridma sat together sharing tea and memories, their lives having transformed dramatically over the past three months. The soft glow of sunset filtered through the windows as Ridma's eyes sparkled with excitement, ready to share her life-changing news.

"Veronica," Ridma began, her voice trembling with joy, "Kavish is being transferred to his hometown at the month's end. We've decided not to wait – we're getting married on the 20th." Her hands wrapped tightly around her teacup as she continued, "It'll be simple, intimate, and just family. Then we'll start our new life in his hometown together."

Veronica reached across the table to squeeze her friend's hand, her heart full of happiness. As they discussed the wedding plans, Ridma's eyes twinkled with mischief. "You know, Veronica... what if you and Vihan got married the same day? Can you imagine how perfect that would be?"

The suggestion left Veronica's mind racing with possibilities. Just days ago, her parents had voiced concerns about rushing into marriage, suggesting that it would be better to take some time to really get to know each other. But deep down, her heart knew what it wanted.

"My parents want me to take more time with Vihan," she admitted, swirling her tea thoughtfully. "But I love him, Ridma. I really do. And imagining our wedding day... it feels like something out of a fairy tale."

The next evening, beneath the soft glow of the cozy coffee shop's lights, Veronica sat across from Vihan, her heart racing with excitement and nervousness. They'd been talking for hours, sharing stories, laughing at memories, but now, her mind was focused on something important. She couldn't stop thinking about Ridma and Kavish's upcoming wedding—scheduled for the 20th. The idea had been swirling in her mind all week, and now, sitting here with Vihan, she knew it was the right time to bring it up.

Her fingers nervously drummed on her coffee cup as she took a deep breath, gathering her courage. "Vihan," she started, her voice slightly trembling, "I've been thinking about something. I know we've talked about marriage, but after hearing Ridma and Kavish set their date for the 20th... I couldn't help but wonder..." She paused, meeting his gaze, unsure of how he would react.

Vihan tilted his head, intrigued, his expression soft and attentive. "What are you thinking?"

Veronica smiled a little, the idea taking shape in her mind as she spoke. "What if we got married on the same day as them? It's a little unconventional, but it feels like it could be... perfect. It would be special, don't you think? Sharing that day with them, but also making it ours."

Vihan blinked in surprise for a moment, and then his face lit up with a mix of excitement and disbelief. "You're serious?" he asked, leaning forward, his voice full of wonder. "You want to get married on the same day as Ridma and Kavish?"

She nodded, a spark of hope in her eyes. "Why not? It's already such a meaningful day for everyone. And sharing it with them could be a beautiful way to start our future together. It might be fast, but with everything we've been through... it feels right."

Vihan leaned back in his chair, processing the suggestion. His eyes searched hers, a mixture of emotions flickering across his face. Then, a slow smile spread across his lips. "You know what? I think I love that idea. It's unique, it's ours, and it feels like it's meant to be."

Her heart skipped a beat at his response. "Really?" she asked, her voice full of hope.

"Really," he said with a grin, his eyes gleaming with excitement. "I've never been one to do things the conventional way, and if we're going to start our lives together, why not make it a day to remember, right? Let's do it."

Veronica's smile stretched across her face, her chest swelling with joy. She reached across the table, taking his hand. "I'm so glad you feel the same way."

With that, they sat there, hand in hand, the future suddenly feeling a little more certain. The idea of getting married on the same day as Ridma and Kavish now felt like the perfect beginning, a shared moment of love and commitment that would mark the start of their new chapter.

The wedding day arrived, bathed in the soft glow of early morning sunlight, as if the universe itself had conspired to make everything perfect. The small hall, once ordinary and unremarkable, had been transformed into a breathtaking oasis, each corner adorned with delicate flowers and twinkling fairy lights. The air was filled with the sweet scent of roses, jasmine, and lavender, their vibrant colors creating a picturesque backdrop for the most important day of their lives.

As guests filtered in, the atmosphere buzzed with laughter, excitement, and a sense of anticipation. Close family and friends gathered, their faces alight with joy, eager to witness this beautiful, shared moment. Two couples, united by love, but each with their own story, were about to take this leap together. Veronica and Vihan stood on one side, Ridma and Kavish on the other, but despite the two ceremonies taking place, the energy in the room was beautifully unified, as if the day belonged to all of them.

The music began, soft and elegant, as the couples made their way to the altar. The hall fell into a respectful hush, eyes glued to the couples who were about to exchange vows. Veronica's heart fluttered as she stood beside Vihan, her hand gripping his, knowing that this day would forever bind them together.

She couldn't help but glance over at Ridma and Kavish, their beaming smiles mirroring her own excitement. It was surreal to see them, two best friends, walking this path together—two couples, one love-filled day.

When the time came to speak their vows, the room seemed to hold its breath. Veronica's voice was steady but full of emotion as she spoke her promises to Vihan. Her words flowed naturally, as if they had been written in her heart long ago, a reflection of everything she had learned about love and commitment. Vihan's gaze never left her, his eyes shining with unspeakable emotion as he spoke his vows in return. Each word was a promise, each sentence a step toward the future they had dreamed of together. The room filled with the energy of their love, and every word seemed to hang in the air, weaving an invisible thread between their hearts.

Next, it was Ridma and Kavish's turn. Their vows, equally heartfelt and sincere, echoed the sentiment that had been building in the room. As Ridma looked at Kavish, the love and trust in her eyes was palpable, and Kavish, ever the playful but deeply sincere partner, spoke with a warmth that brought a smile to everyone's face. It was clear that their love story had led them to this moment, and the bond between them was just as strong as that of Veronica and Vihan.

As the ceremonies came to a close, the air was thick with joy, love, and promise. Both couples stood together, hands entwined, as the officiants declared them officially married. The room erupted into applause, the air charged with an overwhelming sense of happiness. Laughter filled the space as guests congratulated the newlyweds, hugs and kisses exchanged, and a sense of peace settled over everyone.

For Veronica and Vihan, this was the beginning of a new chapter, one filled with hope, love, and the promise of a future together. And for Ridma and Kavish, it was a new beginning too, a day they would always look back on as the moment their lives together truly began.

The day, a beautiful union of two couples, felt like something out of a fairy tale—two ceremonies, one perfect day, shared love, and memories that would last a lifetime. The world outside might have continued to spin, but for that moment, it felt like time had stood still, allowing them to savor the beauty of the present and the love they would carry into their shared futures.

Three months into their marriage, life had settled into a beautiful rhythm. The early days of newness had melted away, replaced by a deeper connection and understanding. Veronica and Vihan found joy in the smallest of moments, those fleeting instances that made their hearts swell with happiness. Morning coffee, still warm from the pot, shared in comfortable silence as they planned their days. Evening walks, hand in hand, their footsteps in sync as they strolled through the quiet streets, content just to be in each other's company. And late nights, lying in bed, whispering about their hopes and dreams for the future, each word a promise of the life they were building together.

Vihan's career was soaring too. After his recent promotion to Marketing Manager at his export company, life seemed even more promising. He had been given a new car—a sleek, dark blue BMW—thanks to his promotion, a symbol of his hard work and dedication.

It was a beautiful gift from the company, and Vihan couldn't help but feel a surge of pride every time he got behind the wheel. He would pick Veronica up from work in the mornings, and they would drive home together, the car's smooth hum matching the rhythm of their life together. Their shared commutes became just another part of their bond, another moment in which they connected. The car, which they jokingly called *The Blue Dream*, had become a symbol of their shared success.

Their home had become a sanctuary, a place where they could simply *be*. The hectic pace of their workdays was always softened by the comfort of being together at night, the world outside forgotten as they spent time together. They hadn't yet reached the stage of life where routines felt monotonous; instead, each day felt like a new adventure. They'd talk about starting a family, the way their home might look with the laughter of children filling the rooms, and all the dreams they had for the future.

But then, one morning, everything changed.

Veronica woke that morning with an unfamiliar queasiness in her stomach, a sensation that unsettled her in ways she couldn't quite explain. It wasn't the usual morning grogginess she'd grown accustomed to after a long day at work. This felt different—persistent, and somehow, a little more intense. She tried to shake it off at first, thinking it might just be stress from the busy week or the heavy workload, but as the hours passed, the unease only grew.

She shared her concern with Vihan over breakfast, her hands nervously stirring her coffee. Vihan, ever the supportive partner, immediately suggested they visit the doctor. The thought of something being wrong was far from their minds, but the nagging feeling wouldn't let them ignore it.

The doctor's office was busy, but Veronica's mind was elsewhere. As they sat in the sterile, quiet room, waiting for the doctor to arrive, her nerves began to settle. Vihan reached across the small table, gently taking her hand in his, offering silent reassurance. The moments ticked by, and soon, the door opened with the doctor stepping in, her professional smile easing the tension in the room.

After a few tests and some quick questions, the doctor glanced up from her clipboard, her smile broadening as she met Veronica's gaze. "Congratulations, Veronica," she said warmly. "You're pregnant."

For a moment, Veronica didn't move, and Vihan just stared, his heart pounding in his chest. The world outside the small room seemed to vanish as the news sank in. Expecting. It was a word that held so much promise, so many dreams for the future, but it also carried a weight of responsibility and change. They had always talked about starting a family, but now that it was real, the reality was more overwhelming and beautiful than either of them had imagined. Veronica felt tears well up, her emotions a whirlwind of joy, surprise, and love. She looked at Vihan, whose eyes were just as wide, his lips trembling with disbelief and happiness.

It took a few moments for the doctor to bring them back to the present as she explained the details, but neither of them truly heard much after that. All that mattered was the word they had just heard: expecting. They were going to be parents.

But life wasn't done surprising them yet.

A few months later, during a routine checkup, they returned to the same doctor's office, a little more relaxed but equally eager to hear the next steps in her pregnancy. Veronica's belly was beginning to show now, and Vihan had been incredibly attentive, always by her side as they navigated this new chapter together.

As the doctor performed the ultrasound, her face lit up with a smile that left Veronica curious and slightly anxious. The room filled with a soft, rhythmic sound—the heartbeat of her baby. But just as they were soaking in the moment, the doctor's expression shifted with a subtle crinkle of delight in her eyes.

"Well, I have some more wonderful news for you both," she said, looking between Veronica and Vihan. "It looks like you're not just expecting one child... but two."

The words hit like a tidal wave, the shock and awe sweeping over them both. Twins. They were going to be parents to two little ones.

Veronica let out a breath she didn't know she'd been holding, her hand instinctively going to her stomach. She exchanged a stunned look with Vihan, whose face broke into a wide grin, his eyes glistening with a mix of amazement and joy. Twins. The future they had imagined had just multiplied, doubling the excitement, the love, and the possibilities.

"We're having twins?" Vihan whispered, as if testing the words to see if they were real.

The doctor nodded, her eyes warm with happiness. "Yes. Congratulations again. It's going to be a wonderful journey for you both."

The room seemed to spin for a moment, and Veronica clutched Vihan's hand tighter, overwhelmed by the news. Their lives were changing in ways they had never imagined. They were about to become parents, and now they would have double the joy, double the responsibility, and double the love to share.

They left the doctor's office that day with their hearts full, their hands joined tightly together, knowing that the life they had been building together had just expanded in the most beautiful, unexpected way. The adventure ahead was even more exciting than they had ever dreamed.

As the reality of expecting twins began to settle in, their home was filled with an energy of preparation and anticipation. What started as a surprise quickly turned into a whirlwind of excitement. Vihan, initially caught off guard by the news, soon found himself deep in planning mode. Despite the thrill, there were moments when he would pause, eyes wide, as he imagined handling two infants at once. The thought of sleepless nights and double the responsibility had him on edge at times, but his joy far outweighed any anxiety.

Veronica's parents, thrilled by the news, dove in headfirst to help. Their enthusiasm was contagious as they transformed the spare room into a warm and welcoming nursery. Every corner was filled with love and care, a safe haven for their soon-to-arrive babies. Veronica found herself sitting in the nursery at night, gently stroking her growing belly, speaking softly to the little ones as if they could already hear her. Vihan, often coming in to check on her, would sit beside her, joining in the quiet conversations. There was an unspoken bond between them, a quiet understanding as they both dreamed about their future.

The love they had found together, beginning with a simple encounter and a twist of fate, had blossomed into something deeper and more beautiful than either of them could have ever imagined. Their relationship had weathered its challenges and now, with the impending arrival of their twin babies, life seemed to be unfolding in the most miraculous way.

Each day brought new joys and challenges, and with each new revelation, they felt more and more blessed. The universe had doubled their blessings in a way that felt both fitting and right – a reward for two hearts that had found each other against all odds. As they navigated this new chapter, their bond only grew stronger, a partnership ready to face the adventure of parenthood. The future, with its unknowns and its promises, was ahead of them, and together, they were ready to embrace it with love, strength, and gratitude.

Chapter 5:

The Roses Torn Apart

Joy radiated from Veronica's face as she gazed down at her newborn twin daughters, their tiny features perfect in every way. Each breath they took, each flutter of their delicate eyelashes, felt like a miracle. Their rosy cheeks and button noses were masterpieces of nature's artistry. Beside her, Vihan stood in silent wonder, his eyes filled with pride as he watched his little family.

"You know," he said, breaking the peaceful silence with a gentle laugh, "we can't keep calling them 'the twins' forever. They need names that are as special as they are."

Veronica smiled, her fingers tracing the soft curve of her daughter's cheek. "I've been thinking about that too. For this little one," she said, looking at the baby in her arms, "what do you think of 'Liana'? It means 'to bind' – like how she's bound our hearts together even more tightly."

Watching Vihan's face soften at the suggestion made her heart swell. "And for her sister," she continued, her voice thick with emotion, "I was thinking of 'Roselle' – my little rose."

"Liana and Roselle," Vihan repeated softly, testing how the names felt on his tongue. "They're perfect. Just like them."

The days that followed were filled with pure bliss. Their home became a sanctuary of baby giggles and tender moments. Veronica threw herself completely into motherhood, leaving her career behind without hesitation. Every midnight feeding, every tiny milestone became a treasure she held close to her heart.

Paradise, it seemed, was built on shifting sands.

Three months had passed since the twins were born, and Veronica had dedicated herself fully to their care. She had left her job, determined not to neglect her precious daughters for even a second. Every moment was spent nurturing and bonding with them, while Vihan continued his work, as he always had. But as the days stretched into weeks, a subtle shift began to take root in their home.

At first, Veronica thought she might be imagining things. The small signs were easy to ignore—the late nights, the vague explanations, the way Vihan seemed distracted when he was home. She brushed it off, convincing herself that it was just the stress of parenthood, the exhaustion of balancing work, life, and their newborns. But the unease in her heart grew, and soon, the changes in Vihan became too obvious to ignore.

His once-warm gaze when he looked at her had grown distant, colder. The connection they had shared seemed to be slipping away. She told herself it was just stress, just the pressures of work, and that things would get better once they adjusted to life with two babies. But something was different. Something felt off, and every time she tried to reach out, to bridge the growing gap between them, it only seemed to widen.

One night, as they sat alone at the dining table, Veronica could no longer hold it in. The tension had built up inside her, and her heart pounded as she spoke. "Vihan, you've changed. I've noticed it," she said softly, her voice steady but heavy with the weight of her fears. "Please, tell me if there's something wrong. If there's something you can't tell me... I want to listen." She paused, searching his eyes for any hint of reassurance. "You've been coming home late more often. It's becoming too frequent, and I don't know what to make of it. You say it's work stress, but... it doesn't feel right."

Vihan's eyes avoided hers, his response distant. "Just work stress, that's all." His words felt empty, lacking the sincerity that once defined them.

Veronica felt a cold shiver run through her, the unease in her chest tightening. His love for their twins was unquestionable, but the love between them—their bond—seemed to be fading. The more she tried to ignore it, the more her gut told her something was terribly wrong.

But the truth, when it finally emerged, shattered her world in ways she couldn't have imagined. Her father, noticing her growing anxiety, had quietly investigated, and what he uncovered turned everything upside down.

Vihan had been hiding something, or rather, someone. Another woman. Another life. A secret world he had been building behind Veronica's back.

The confrontation that followed was a whirlwind of emotions—shock, disbelief, rage, and heartbreak all tangled into one. Veronica's voice shook as she cried out, "How could you, Vihan? How could you betray us like this? We have a family... we have our beautiful daughters!"

Vihan's words cut deeper than any knife. His face, usually so calm and collected, was now filled with a mixture of frustration and bitterness. "You stopped seeing me, Veronica. Ever since the twins came, I've been nothing but a shadow in this house. It's like I don't even exist anymore." His voice was raw, pained, but it was the truth, as twisted as it was.

The argument escalated, their voices rising in a fury of hurt and anger, until the sound of the twins crying from their nursery pierced the air. Veronica's heart twisted in anguish, but it was the words that followed that would haunt her forever.

"I'm leaving," Vihan declared, his voice icy, devoid of any warmth. "And I'm taking Roselle with me."

Time seemed to freeze. The air thickened, and Veronica's world turned into a blur of panic. "No!" she screamed, her heart crashing in her chest. She lunged forward, desperate to reach him, to stop him from taking their daughter. "You can't take my baby, Vihan! Please, don't do this!" Her voice broke, pleading, begging for him to stay, but it was like she was speaking to a stranger.

The reality of it all hit her like a tidal wave. She had never imagined a moment like this. The man she had loved, the man she had built a life with, was walking away. And with him, he was taking the one thing that mattered most—their daughter.

But her pleas fell on deaf ears. In a blur of motion and tears, Vihan scooped up Roselle and walked out the door, leaving Veronica collapsed on the floor, clutching Liana to her chest as though she might disappear too.

The night that followed was the longest of Veronica's life. Her parents rushed to her side, but nothing could ease the agony of having half her heart torn away. Liana's cries echoed through the house, as if she too could feel the absence of her twin sister.

As dawn broke, Veronica stood at her window, Liana sleeping fitfully in her arms. Her tears had dried, replaced by a steel-like determination. "I promise you, my sweet girl," she whispered, pressing a kiss to Liana's forehead, "I will bring your sister home. No matter what it takes, no matter how long it takes, I will make our family whole again."

Looking up at the first rays of sunlight breaking through the clouds, Veronica made a silent vow. This wasn't the end of their story – it was just the beginning of her fight to reunite her precious roses, torn apart by betrayal but bound forever by love.

The road ahead would be long and difficult, but Veronica knew that somewhere out there, Roselle was waiting for her mother to bring her home. And nothing – not distance, not time, not even Vihan's betrayal – would stop her from making that happen.

Chapter 6:

The Unexpected Reunion

After Vihan disappeared from Veronica's life, leaving a trail of heartache, she had no choice but to pull herself together and rebuild from the ground up. With a steady job to support herself and her baby, Liana, Veronica threw herself into the chaos of work and motherhood. It wasn't easy, but thankfully, her parents, Gerald and Clara, became her rock. They absolutely adored their granddaughter and took on their new roles as caregivers with open arms, cherishing every moment with her while Veronica was at work.

But as Liana grew, her vibrant personality started to show itself in all its glory—equal parts delightful and downright mischievous. She became known for her stubbornness and her fierce independence, never one to follow the rules or bend to anyone's advice. When her mother was home, Liana transformed into the most angelic little girl you could imagine, aware of Veronica's more disciplined nature. But as soon as Veronica was out the door, Liana took full advantage of her grandparents' endless love and patience, making sure they knew she was in charge.

Gerald and Clara often laughed off Liana's antics, chalking them up to typical childhood behavior. They preferred to focus on her adorable moments, avoiding telling Veronica just how tricky her daughter could be. But Veronica, being a mom, could tell. Liana was a handful—hard to control and even harder to predict.

One thing was for sure—mealtimes with Liana were always an adventure.

"No, Nana! Don't put broccoli on my plate!" she would whine, pushing the offending vegetable away with the dramatic flair of a diva. Clara, already prepared for the fight, would offer a solution: "Liana, sweetheart, just one bite. It'll make you big and strong, like a superhero!"

Liana, with a defiant puff of her chest, would respond, "I'm already a superhero!" before zooming around the room, pretending to fly like the best of them.

Gerald, always the peacemaker, would step in with a little puppet dance to distract her. Liana would giggle uncontrollably as he made funny faces and twirled around like a goofy entertainer. Seizing the moment, Clara would quickly sneak in a spoonful of food while Liana was distracted. She wouldn't even notice until it was too late.

But mealtimes were just the beginning. One afternoon, Gerald was napping on the couch, when Liana, never one to miss an opportunity, decided Grandpa needed a makeover. Armed with her coloring box, she covered his face in bright markers—curly mustaches, thick eyebrows, and a few artistic flourishes for good measure, just like she'd seen Veronica do when applying makeup. When Clara walked in and saw the masterpiece, she couldn't help but gasp, her lips trembling with laughter.

"Liana! What have you done to Grandpa?" Clara exclaimed, trying—and failing—to keep a straight face.

Liana looked up with an innocent grin and said, "Grandpa looks handsome with this painting!"

Gerald, waking up from his nap, blinked in confusion before catching a glimpse of himself in the mirror. He stared at his newly decorated face and shook his head, part-scolding, part-laughing. "Liana, you little rascal! What am I going to do with you?"

With a hearty laugh, he added, "She's the boss around here, that's for sure," before pulling Liana into a big hug. "And we wouldn't have it any other way."

Despite all her mischief, Liana had a way of melting their hearts with her infectious spirit. Life with her was never dull, and though she was the boss, Gerald and Clara couldn't imagine a more perfect whirlwind of chaos to share their days with.

When Liana turned five, Veronica decided it was time for her to start school. She enrolled her daughter at St. Grace's City Girls College, a prestigious institution known for its excellent discipline and academic standards. Every morning, Veronica would drop Liana off before heading to work, leaving Gerald to pick her up in the afternoons. But every day, without fail, Gerald would be met with the same complaint from Liana's teacher, Ms. Matilda.

"She's bright," Ms. Matilda would begin, her voice strained with frustration, "but she's also terribly rebellious."

Gerald, already familiar with his granddaughter's fiery spirit, would listen patiently, nodding sympathetically. His eyes, however, often twinkled with amusement at the tales Ms. Matilda shared. "Today, for example," she would continue, "she started a quarrel with an innocent girl just by messing up her neatly arranged pencil box. It's like she can't help stirring up trouble."

"She's the leader of her little rebellion gang," Ms. Matilda added, shaking her head. "She can be charming, but she's got a knack for creating chaos. She's not one to back down, and she always seems to have a plan."

Gerald chuckled, trying to hold back his smile. "Yes, Madam, I can understand. She's a bit stubborn, isn't she?" He gave a knowing look, his tone warm and understanding. "She's gotten used to being the center of attention, with all the love around her. She's just at that age, you know, when mischief becomes second nature."

Ms. Matilda offered a small, approving smile. "I suppose you're right, Gerald. These are mischievous ages, after all. But it's certainly a challenge."

"I'll have a word with her," Gerald said, a glint of mischief in his own eyes. "But you know, I've learned there's not much use in telling her off too much. She's got a hundred reasons to excuse her behavior." He chuckled softly. "I'll approach it in a loving way. No use in making a fuss—she's got a heart of gold, just a bit... spirited."

Ms. Matilda gave a soft laugh, appreciating his perspective, before she left them to go back to her classroom. Gerald sighed but smiled to himself. No matter how many stories he heard, he knew one thing for sure: Liana's determination and spunk would get her far in life. And while it might take some guidance, he was confident she would turn out just fine—rebellious spirit and all.

Liana couldn't stand Roselle. The sweet, soft-spoken girl seemed to embody everything Liana found annoying. Roselle's gentle demeanor and effortless charm won over teachers and classmates alike, making her a favorite wherever she went. But in Liana's eyes, Roselle wasn't someone to admire—she was a rival to despise.

Liana seized every chance to make Roselle's life difficult. During lessons, she would shoot icy glares in her direction. In quieter moments, she'd deliberately knock over Roselle's books or sneak away with her belongings, leaving the poor girl bewildered and hurt. Despite Liana's relentless bullying, Roselle never struck back. Instead, she maintained a quiet resilience, her dignified silence only serving to deepen Liana's frustration.

While Liana enjoyed a loving, if sometimes strict, upbringing with her mother and doting grandparents, Roselle's life was a stark contrast. She lived under the thumb of her stepmother, Alina—a woman whose breathtaking beauty was rivaled only by her cold and calculating nature.

Alina ruled her household with an iron fist, her obsession with perfection making her harsh and demanding. One evening, her sharp voice cut through the silence of their home. "Roselle! Did you finish cleaning the living room?"

"Yes, Mom," Roselle answered softly, her fingers nervously clutching the hem of her dress.

"Then get to scrubbing the floors! They're a disgrace!" Alina barked, her tone laced with irritation.

Vihan, aware of Alina's relentless cruelty, often tried to step in. "Alina, she's just a child. You don't have to be so hard on her," he said, his voice firm yet pleading.

Alina rolled her eyes dramatically, her expression one of complete indifference. "Oh, spare me, Vihan," she snapped. "If she's living under my roof, she'll follow my rules."

Roselle said nothing, quietly obeying as always, her kind spirit shining through despite the harsh environment she endured.

Despite her stepmother's harsh treatment, Roselle never complained. Her deep love for her father kept her from stirring up trouble. She couldn't shake the feeling that her father was under his wife's influence, likely due to her considerable wealth.

Ironically, Vihan and Veronica crossed paths every day at the school without realizing it, as they dropped off their daughters at different times. Fate, however, was about to intervene in an unexpected way.

One day, during a classmate's birthday celebration, Sophia brought a large cake to share with the class. Ms. Matilda carefully cut it into slices and distributed them to the students. As Roselle quietly held her piece, savoring the moment, Liana marched over with a smug grin and snatched it from her hands.

"Hey! That's mine!" Roselle exclaimed, her voice trembling with frustration as she reached for her piece.

Liana's eyes glinted mischievously. "Not anymore," she sneered, taking a step back. "You don't deserve it." She paused, a cruel smile spreading across her face. "If you're brave enough, try to get it back from me."

The situation quickly escalated into a full-blown argument, with the two girls pushing and shoving each other in a heated fight. Ms. Matilda, her patience clearly running thin, stepped in with authority, her voice cutting through the noise and immediately silencing the classroom.

"That's enough! Both of you!" she commanded, her eyes blazing with anger. "You will both be punished. Go to the storeroom, now. You'll stay there until the end of school, and I will lock the door."

The storeroom was small and dimly lit, its musty air pressing in around the girls as they sat in opposite corners, seething with anger. The silence hung thick between them, broken only by the occasional sound of a breath or a shift in position. Finally, Liana, unable to contain her fury, spoke first, her voice low but filled with resentment.

"This is your fault!" she snapped. "If you hadn't reacted, we wouldn't be here!"

"It's my piece of cake," Roselle shot back, her voice steady but firm. "Why did you try to take it?"

The argument fizzled out as exhaustion set in. They sat quietly, each lost in their thoughts, until Roselle noticed something moving in the shadows. Her eyes widened in horror.

"Liana," she whispered urgently. "Don't move."

"What now?" Liana groaned.

"There's a snake... right next to you!"

Liana froze, her face pale with fear. Before she could react, Roselle sprang into action, grabbing Liana's arm and pulling her to safety. The snake slithered away through a crack in the wall, leaving the girls breathless.

"You... you saved me," Liana stammered, her voice tinged with disbelief.

"Of course I did," Roselle replied, her voice soft. "I couldn't let anything happen to you."

For the first time, Liana looked at Roselle with a new sense of recognition. There was something about her—something she couldn't quite put her finger on—that made her feel oddly familiar.

"You're... you're nice," Liana said, her voice softening as she spoke the words reluctantly. "Even when I've been horrible to you."

Roselle, unfazed, met her gaze with a calm smile. "I don't think you're really horrible," she replied, her voice gentle. "I think you're just... misunderstood. You're smart, Liana. I can see that."

Liana stared at her, a thought beginning to form. "We look alike," she said slowly. "Like... exactly alike."

"I noticed that too," Roselle replied, her voice filled with wonder. "Do you think we could be... sisters?"

Liana's mind raced as she remembered the many times her mother had mentioned she had a twin sister, how her father had taken her away during one of their arguments, and how her mother always avoided talking about him afterward. "Maybe we are," she whispered, her voice barely audible.

"If we are," Roselle said, her eyes sparkling with a hint of hope, "don't you want to know the truth?"

Liana's heart skipped a beat, and for a moment, she was lost in the possibility. She had so many questions, so many things she wanted to understand. Then, a mischievous grin slowly spread across her face, and her eyes gleamed with determination.

"Oh, I do," she said, her voice dripping with excitement. "And I've got a plan."

Roselle blinked, curiosity flooding her expression. "A plan? What kind of plan?"

Liana leaned in closer, her voice dropping to a whisper, brimming with excitement. "A plan to uncover everything. We'll find out who we really are, and maybe... just maybe, we'll get to meet the parents who've kept us apart all this time."

Roselle's breath caught in her throat, a mixture of excitement and nerves swirling inside her. Could this really be happening? Could they truly find the answers they both longed for? She nodded, a soft smile tugging at her lips.

"I'm in," she whispered.

Liana and Roselle quickly swapped their school uniforms, shoes, and bags, each carefully adjusting to the other's style as they prepared for their new roles. Liana smiled as she zipped up Roselle's bag, noting the small details that seemed so different from her own.

Roselle took a deep breath and began, her voice low but clear. "When my dad comes to pick me up, you'll know it's him by the silver car with tinted windows. He always parks right by the school gate." She paused, her eyes meeting Liana's with a touch of seriousness. "At home, I need to follow everything my stepmother, Alina says, even if it doesn't feel right. She's strict about the house being perfect—cleaning, cooking, everything. It's like walking on eggshells."

Liana nodded, processing everything Roselle shared before offering her own updates. "At my place, it's mostly my grandpa and grandma who take care of me. Mom's always working, so they feel like my second parents. Grandpa is hilarious, always trying to make me laugh when I'm being picky about food. Grandma... she's kind, but she can be pretty strict at mealtimes. As for Mom, she's a bit tough on me, but I know she loves me."

They looked at each other for a moment, a sense of readiness settling in. "We're ready," Liana said with a determined grin.

Roselle smiled back, her nerves giving way to excitement. "Let's do this."

And just like that, they were ready for the task ahead—two girls, now prepared to step into each other's worlds and uncover the secrets that had kept them apart.

Chapter 7:

A Day of New Beginnings

Later that afternoon, the school bell rang, signaling the end of the day.

Liana stood nervously by the school gate, clutching her bag and glancing at every passing car. Roselle had told her all the details—"Look for a silver car with tinted windows. He's tall and usually wears a white shirt. Don't be scared." But no matter how much Liana had prepared herself, she couldn't shake the nervous flutter in her chest.

Finally, the car pulled up. It was exactly as Roselle had described, and the man in the driver's seat fit her description perfectly. Swallowing her nerves, Liana ran toward the car.

The man looked surprised as she dashed up to the passenger side and climbed in with a bright smile.

"Hi, Daddy!" she said, trying her best to sound cheerful and confident.

He blinked in surprise, his eyes narrowing as he took in Roselle's energetic approach. Normally, she would quietly walk over and greet him with a simple "Hi, Dad." But today, she was running to the car and now staring at him as if he were a stranger. "What's going on, Roselle? Running to the car like that, and now you're looking at me like you don't know me. Are you feeling alright?"

Liana felt her heart race. She forced a casual laugh. "Oh, nothing! Today we got homework—to write an essay about our daddy. I just... wanted to get a good image of you in my mind!"

He chuckled, though there was a flicker of doubt in his eyes. "Well, that's... sweet, I suppose. But you're acting a little strange today. Are you sure you're okay?"

"Yes, Daddy, I'm fine!" she replied quickly, looking away to avoid his gaze. Her heart was pounding. Would he figure it out?

On the other side, Roselle stood quietly by the school gate, her bag clutched tightly in her hands. She didn't have to wait long before she spotted the Grandpa, Gerald's figure in the distance. As he approached, his usual warm smile lit up his face, instantly easing her nerves.

But instead of handing him her bag as Liana usually did, Roselle ran toward him with a bright, genuine grin on her face. She placed her small hand into his, her eyes sparkling with excitement.

Gerald was surprised by her sudden change but kept quiet for a moment. However, as they walked toward the bus stop, he couldn't hold it in any longer. With a teasing smile, he turned to Liana—though it was actually Roselle—and asked, "Have you left your chatterbox behind? No complaints about carrying your bag? No demands for sweets on the way?"

Roselle giggled, her eyes twinkling. "No, Grandpa. I'm just happy to see you."

He gave her an affectionate pat on the head, though he couldn't help but notice her behavior was different. Usually, his granddaughter was a whirlwind of stubborn demands and endless chatter. But today, she was quiet, polite, and even a little shy.

"Well, well," he said as they walked home. "I think our little girl is finally growing up. Learning the difference between good and bad, eh?"

Roselle just smiled, her heart warm. It felt strange but wonderful to hold his hand and feel his love. The tender care from her grandpa had soothed her, giving her a sense of belonging she had never felt before. Yet, a pang of envy stirred within her for Liana—the life of love and warmth she had experienced. It was everything Roselle had longed for, everything she had missed. How lucky Liana was to have a family that showered her with affection. But today was different. Today, Roselle was going to meet the woman she had dreamed of—her real mother, Veronica. A figure in her life.

The moment Roselle saw Veronica arrive home from work, her heart skipped a beat. Her eyes widened in disbelief, and before she could think, she flung her arms wide and ran toward her. Each step was filled with the weight of years of longing, the deep yearning to finally bridge the gap and feel the connection she had always dreamed of.

The embrace that followed was overwhelming. Veronica's arms enveloped her with a tenderness that Roselle had never known. The world around them seemed to pause as she melted into the warmth of her mother's presence. The scent of her, the feeling of her arms around her, was more than Roselle could bear. This was the woman who had carried her in her heart despite the years of separation, the silence, the longing.

Veronica, her eyes wide with a mix of surprise and awe, couldn't help but be taken aback by the intensity of Liana's reaction. There was something undeniably profound, something intensely emotional in the way the girl clung to her—far more than Veronica had ever anticipated. It was raw, powerful, and deeply touching.

Veronica, still a bit taken aback by the sudden display of affection, finally spoke, her voice a mix of concern and curiosity. "Liana, you're so sweet today. How was school? Did you get along well?"

Roselle's voice trembled, filled with emotion as the weight of everything she had experienced over the past months poured into a single sentence. "It was... wonderful," she whispered, her words laced with sincerity. In that moment, all the confusion, the unanswered questions, and the loneliness seemed to fade away. Roselle had found her place. She had found her home.

Veronica smiled warmly, her expression a blend of relief and happiness. She kissed Liana's forehead, her hand gently brushing through her hair. Unaware that it was Roselle, she savored the moment—the bond between them—something deeper and more meaningful than she could have ever imagined.

"Well, let's sit down and have something to eat." Veronica glanced at the dishes on the table and smiled warmly. "Liana, your grandma made your favorite," she added, her voice tender and full of affection. To Roselle, it wasn't just an invitation; it was a promise of love, safety, and acceptance. This was it. This was home.

As Veronica and Liana shared a meal, Gerald stood in the doorway, quietly watching with a heart full of pride and contentment. He had witnessed this child's remarkable transformation—how she had begun to bloom under the loving care of her grandparents. Seeing her progress, gaining confidence, and growing in ways that were becoming more and more apparent to those around her brought him a deep sense of relief. The change was undeniable, and for the first time in a long while, he felt a genuine hope for her future.

"Maybe school really has done some good after all," Gerald thought to himself, observing the tender moment between Veronica and Liana, unaware that it was Roselle. As he watched, a deep sense of gratitude washed over him for the place that had helped guide her through the difficult times. But more than that, he felt an overwhelming sense of hope.

Roselle was finally on the right path. She had found her family, and now, perhaps, she was beginning to find herself.

When Liana arrived at Vihan's house, her eyes were immediately drawn to his second wife, Alina, standing at the door. Alina exuded a stylish, almost regal aura, her presence unmistakable and commanding. But the moment she spotted Liana, her attention shifted, locking onto the girl before her with a piercing gaze.

"Roselle, hurry up and have your lunch, then wash everything in the sink and clean the kitchen," Alina ordered, her tone sharp and commanding. "Don't just stand there."

Liana wasn't used to that kind of commanding tone at all. It made her furious, but she managed to control her anger, reminding herself of Roselle's advice to stay calm and not draw attention—after all, their plan depended on it.

As she ate her lunch, Liana thought to herself, *I'll teach her a good lesson soon, no matter what Roselle says or does.* She couldn't help but feel that this nasty woman had been spoiled beyond measure.

Since it was her first day, Liana decided to follow her orders, though not with the same precision Roselle would. Once again, Alina snapped at her. Liana blinked in surprise, unaccustomed to being spoken to like this. She glanced at Vihan, hoping for some support, but he only looked away, his expression distant and helpless.

She muttered to herself, "Don't worry, Dad. You'll see tomorrow what happens to her. I'll teach her a good lesson." With that, she returned to her chores, her mind already plotting what was to come.

The next afternoon, after another successful exchange of homes, Liana sat at the dining table, enjoying a quick lunch after school. Her eyes followed Alina as she moved briskly around the kitchen, her demeanor as commanding as ever. Moments later, Alina returned and handed Liana a list of chores for the day—sweeping, washing dishes, folding laundry, and a seemingly endless list of tasks.

Liana frowned, gripping her spoon tightly. She had had enough.

"Why are you always giving me these chores?" Liana said, her voice sharper than usual. "I have my studies to do. You think I'm here to be your maid?"

Alina stopped mid-step, turning to face her. "Excuse me? What did you just say?"

"You heard me," Liana said, rising to her feet and locking eyes with Alina. "If you keep trying to boss me around, I'll teach you a lesson you'll never forget. Don't think I'm still the innocent, timid girl you can push around anymore."

Alina's eyebrows shot up, clearly stunned. She wasn't used to Roselle—or who she thought was Roselle—talking back. What?? How dare you speak to me like that?" Alina snapped, placing her hands on her hips. "You're just a child. I run this house, and you'll do as I say."

Liana smirked, leaning back against the chair. "Run this house? That's funny because all I see is you barking orders while doing nothing. Let me make this clear—if you don't stop, you'll regret it."

Alina scoffed. "And what exactly are you going to do, little brat?"

Without missing a beat, Liana grabbed a nearby broomstick and held it up, her eyes blazing. "You see this? If you don't clean this house yourself today, I'll make sure you understand what I'm capable of. Try me."

Alina's face paled, the usual confidence draining from her features. She took a step back, glancing nervously at the broomstick. "You wouldn't dare," she said, but her voice lacked conviction.

"Oh, wouldn't I?" Liana said, twirling the broomstick casually in her hand. "Your move."

Defeated and clearly intimidated, Alina grabbed a dust cloth and started dusting the shelves, muttering under her breath. Liana watched her with a satisfied grin before settling down in the armchair with a novel.

As Alina scrubbed the floor, she glanced over at Liana, who was lounging comfortably, flipping through the pages of her book. It was a scene Vihan walked into when he returned home later that day.

"What's going on here?" Vihan asked, his voice filled with confusion.

Alina, sweating and red-faced, stood up quickly. "Nothing! Just cleaning the house," she said, plastering on a fake smile.

But Vihan's eyes darted to Liana, who was still seated in the armchair, seemingly unconcerned. "And you? Since when do you relax while others clean?"

Liana shrugged, her expression nonchalant. "She told me to do her chores earlier, so I told her to do them herself. Fair's fair, isn't it?"

Vihan frowned. This was strange. Roselle—at least who he thought was Roselle—was always quiet, obedient, and never one to argue back, let alone delegate chores to someone like Alina. Something felt off.

He pulled Alina aside later that evening. "What's going on with her?" he asked. "She's been acting...different lately."

Alina huffed, crossing her arms. "You think I know? All I know is she's suddenly rebellious and bold. Honestly, it's annoying."

Vihan didn't respond immediately, his mind racing. "I'm going to the school tomorrow," he muttered, more to himself than to Alina.

"What for?" Alina asked, raising an eyebrow.

"There's something I need to check," Vihan said firmly.

The next morning, as Vihan drove her to school, he glanced at her curiously.

"You seem happier these days," he remarked casually.

“Of course, Daddy,” Liana replied with an unusual confidence in her tone. “Life’s finally getting interesting.”

Her response only heightened his suspicion. By the time they arrived at the school, Vihan was determined to uncover what was really going on.

After Liana went inside the school, Vihan sat in the car, deep in thought. His mind was still tangled with confusion over her strange behavior. He was considering meeting with her class teacher when something caught his eye—a woman walking towards him with a child about Roselle’s age. His heart raced. *My God, that’s Veronica... What on earth is she doing here?*

As Veronica passed by the car, Roselle spotted him and, without thinking, blurted out, "Dad!" Veronica, startled, peered inside the car, her eyes widening in surprise as she saw Vihan staring at her, his expression a mix of shock and confusion.

Veronica stood speechless for a moment, then managed to say, "Vihan, you’re here?"

With a burst of excitement, Roselle flung open the car door, her eyes sparkling with energy. "Dad! It’s me, Roselle!" she exclaimed, her voice full of joy. "I’ve been with my mom all week, and Liana was with you! I finally found my sister!" The words rushed out in a flood, and in that moment, everything felt like it was falling into place.

Vihan and Veronica stood frozen, their mouths hanging open in stunned silence. Veronica tightened her grip on Roselle, her heart racing with a mixture of disbelief and overwhelming joy. "Thank God for this moment," she whispered, her voice thick with emotion. "Where’s Liana?"

Vihan, still trying to process the whirlwind of emotions, blinked in confusion. "She’s already in her classroom."

Veronica gasped, her eyes welling up. "I can’t believe it... I’ve found my two angels."

Before they could fully absorb the moment, Roselle, full of excitement, darted toward the classroom. In an instant, she returned with Liana by her side, and the sisters stood together, beaming with happiness. It was a reunion, a moment of pure magic, as if the world had finally aligned perfectly.

Chapter 8:

The Ties That Bind

The next morning, after dropping Roselle and Liana off at school as planned, Veronica and Vihan met at a small coffee shop. The air was filled with a mix of nervous anticipation and determination as they sat across from each other, the weight of the decision before them heavy in the silence.

After a long and heartfelt conversation, they reached a resolution. It was time to make things right—no more dwelling on the past, but instead, creating a future where their daughters could finally be together. No more hiding the truth, no more living in the shadows. They decided to take their daughters out of school that very day and give them a fun, memorable time.

Vihan paused, his voice faltering as he spoke from the depths of his heart. He looked at Veronica, the regret in his eyes heavier than he could express. "Veronica, please, I need you to understand. I was so caught up in my own foolish desires that I lost sight of what truly mattered. I was blinded by the illusion of wealth and beauty, thinking it would bring me happiness. But in the process, I hurt you, I hurt Roselle... and I made the worst mistake of my life by abandoning you both."

His hands clenched at his sides, as if the weight of his past actions was still too much to bear. "I realize now just how reckless I was.

I was such a fool, Veronica. I chased after something empty, trading real love for a fantasy. The only small mercy is that I never married her - we just lived together. I thought her wealth and pride meant something, but I was just another victim of her games. Even surrounded by comfort and luxury, I was never truly happy there. How could I be? Everything that mattered - real love, trust, our family - I'd left behind with you.

Vihan's eyes lowered for a moment as the pain of the past settled on him again. "I've already told her I'm leaving, and she didn't even care, just said I could go whenever I wanted. Her pride kept her from seeing what I truly needed, which was a chance to rebuild what I ruined. And that's when I realized—it wasn't just about me. It was about Roselle. She's the one who paid the price for my foolishness."

His voice cracked with the weight of his guilt. "I can't bear the thought of her suffering because of my actions. Please, Veronica... I know I can never undo the past, but I swear I'll do everything I can to make things right. If you'll let me, I want to build a future for us, for all of us, and give Roselle and Liana the family they deserve."

The silence that followed was filled with raw emotion, the burden of his mistakes heavy but the hope for redemption shining through his words.

His eyes met hers, heavy with years of regret. For a moment, he just breathed, letting his guard fall completely. "Veronica... the man who hurt you, who made those foolish choices - he's gone. I've changed, truly changed." His voice grew quiet but firm. "I'll speak with Alina. Since we never married, ending things will be straightforward. And knowing her pride, she'll let me go without a fight.

She'd rather walk away with her head high than try to keep someone who doesn't want to stay."He paused, his voice gentle but resolute. "I've hurt you, and I can't undo that, but I want to make things right for our family."

Veronica took a deep breath, her chest rising and falling as the heaviness that had gripped her for so long seemed to lift just a little. Her gaze softened as she met Vihan's, the years of pain and frustration finally finding a release in her words. "Vihan, I admit, I too made mistakes. I neglected you in my own way, without truly thinking about what it would mean for us... for our family," she said, her voice steady but tinged with honesty. "But if you had come to me with your concerns, instead of making harsh decisions, maybe things could have been different. Maybe... they could have been more beautiful."

She paused, a quiet sadness in her eyes as she continued, her tone now filled with both strength and vulnerability. "I don't want to dwell on the pain and emotional turmoil I went through after you left. It was hard, harder than I ever let on. But I've learned that sometimes, it's better to let bygones be bygones. What's done is done."

Veronica's voice grew more determined as she leaned forward slightly, a spark of clarity in her gaze. "Now, we need to focus on what's right—what's best for our two daughters. They deserve better than the past we've given them. They deserve us working together to make things right."

She gave him a reassuring look, her words final but filled with a sense of hope.

"Let's make sure we're both there for them. Let's fix this. We still have the chance to build something good, something that will make all of us stronger."

They sat together, the weight of their conversation lingering in the air, as they carefully discussed their future plans, each word bringing them closer to a mutual understanding. The room felt quieter now, as if the world outside had paused to give them this moment of clarity. As they spoke, their past mistakes and regrets seemed to fade into the background, overshadowed by the realization that there was still hope for a new beginning—a chance to rebuild what had once been broken.

When the conversation came to a natural pause, they both stood up simultaneously, an unspoken agreement passing between them. There was no need for more words. It was as if the very act of standing together, side by side, solidified their resolve. The past was behind them, and ahead lay the path they would walk together, no longer as separate individuals, but as a united family determined to do right by their daughters.

The school loomed ahead of them, its familiar walls seeming different now, imbued with a new sense of possibility. The path before them was uncertain, but there was a quiet certainty in their hearts—an understanding that they were taking the right steps, even if they didn't know exactly what the future held. Their hearts beat in sync, the anticipation of what was to come growing with every step.

As they walked side by side, a sense of peace settled over them. They were no longer carrying the weight of unresolved tension or unspoken regrets. The future, though still unknown, felt like something they could face together, with their daughters as the guiding light that would keep them moving forward. And for the first time in a long time, both Veronica and Vihan felt that the road ahead, no matter how challenging, was one they were ready to walk—together.

When they arrived at the school, Miss Matilda, the warm and approachable class teacher, greeted them with a friendly smile. However, her expression quickly shifted to one of confusion, unable to comprehend what was about to unfold.

Miss Matilda asked the monitor to look after the class and led them to the visitors' room. Vihan allowed Veronica to explain. She took a deep breath, her heart racing with excitement and resolve, and then spoke clearly, her words carrying the weight of the revelation. "Miss Matilda, we need to talk to you about Roselle and Liana. There's been a misunderstanding. They're sisters, and we've just discovered the truth."

The words hung in the air for a moment, and Miss Matilda's eyes widened in shock. "What do you mean? I didn't get it correctly. I'm a bit confused."

Veronica took a deep breath, her eyes steady as she began to explain. "Yes, Miss Matilda. Liana and Roselle are sisters, though they were unaware of each other's existence for many years due to our separation. Liana has been with me, and Roselle with Vihan. When they were infants, circumstances led to their separation, and only recently did they discover the truth.

They've both been in your class all this time, unknowingly sharing the same space, unaware of their connection."

Miss Matilda listened in stunned silence, the pieces of the puzzle clicking into place, though she didn't press further, respecting the personal nature of the matter. "I'm happy that at least they've discovered each other's connection," she said thoughtfully. "Actually, I noticed in the past few days that they've become much friendlier. There were so many private talks between them—I just didn't realize it was because they were sisters."

Veronica nodded, her face brightening with a warm smile as she took a step closer. "I know it's hard to believe. They've spent most of their lives unaware of the truth, and that misunderstanding influenced their actions. But now everything has changed. They're no longer just classmates—now, all four of us are a family."

Miss Matilda's eyes softened, and a gentle smile spread across her face. "I can't express how happy I am for both of you," she said, her voice warm and sincere. It's a beautiful thing, really. A family reunited." "It's not every day that such a beautiful and unexpected reunion happens. To think that Liana and Roselle, after all this time, are finally able to embrace their true connection—it's truly heartwarming."

She paused for a moment, her expression full of admiration. "I can see the bond growing between them already. It's amazing to witness, and I'm so glad they're able to share this new chapter of their lives together. It's a rare gift, and I truly wish them all the happiness in the world."

Her eyes glistened with emotion as she continued, "This kind of love and togetherness is what makes life so precious. I'm honored to have witnessed this part of their journey."

Veronica nodded, her heart overflowing with emotion. "They've finally found each other, and it's been such a beautiful journey for both of them. What we once saw as rivalry was really just the lack of something—love, understanding, and, above all, family." She smiled, a tear threatening to escape, but her pride in the girls' reunion was clear.

"Now that they've discovered the truth, everything feels right. It's like all the pieces finally came together."

Veronica nodded gently, her tone respectful but firm. "Madam, we're planning to take them both home early today. We hope you understand, and we would really appreciate it if you could release them now."

After a brief pause, Miss Matilda smiled, her surprise giving way to understanding. “Well, this is unexpected, but I see. Go ahead and take them, but just a reminder—by the end of the month, their term tests will be here. I hope you can help them stay on track.”

Veronica nodded with a grateful smile. “Yes, Madam, we'll make sure from tomorrow onwards their school attendance will be smooth and punctual. We truly appreciate your understanding and flexibility in this matter. It means a lot to us, and we'll ensure they stay focused and prepared for their tests. Thank you again for your support."

With Miss Matilda's approval, Veronica and Vihan walked into the classroom, their footsteps a little lighter, their hearts filled with excitement. The girls, sitting at their desks, looked up in confusion, their faces blank at first as they tried to make sense of what was happening. A ripple of curiosity passed through them as they saw their parents approaching.

Veronica's eyes locked with Liana's and Roselle's, her voice gentle and filled with warmth. "Liana, Roselle," she called softly, her tone drawing their attention. "It's time for all of us to have some fun."

The words hung in the air for a moment, as the girls exchanged uncertain glances, trying to decipher the sudden shift. But as Veronica smiled at them, the confusion melted away, replaced by an unfamiliar thrill of possibility. For the first time, it felt like everything was aligning, and a new chapter was beginning—one that was full of surprises, unity, and the promise of fun.

Liana's face lit up with a spark of realization, and Roselle's eyes brightened, her hand instinctively reaching for Liana's. In that moment, all the doubts and uncertainties faded into the background. This wasn't just a change—it was a new beginning.

The girls exchanged a glance, their eyes wide with a mix of surprise and wonder. Slowly, they stood and walked toward their parents, an invisible bond pulling them closer. As they reached out, hands trembling slightly, an air of excitement and nervousness hung between them.

Roselle looked up at Veronica, a smile tugging at her lips, her eyes soft with relief. "Are we really going to be together, Mom?" she asked, her voice filled with disbelief and joy.

Veronica's heart swelled as she gently took Roselle's hand. "Yes, sweetheart. We're together now. All of us, as a family."

Liana, still processing the whirlwind of emotions, turned to Vihan, her hand squeezing his tightly. Her eyes shimmered with unshed tears, a mixture of hope and disbelief in her gaze. "I can't believe it," she whispered, her voice breaking the silence.

Vihan's smile was warm and reassuring as he looked at his daughter, his hand resting firmly in hers. "Believe it, Liana," he said softly. "We're going to make things right, starting today."

Together, they stepped out of the classroom, their united steps echoing through the quiet hallways. With each footfall, they left behind the past, stepping boldly into a new chapter—one that promised fresh beginnings, healing, and the joy of a family finally whole.

Chapter Title: 9 Homecoming of Hearts

The air at Veronica's house was charged with an electric excitement, a palpable sense of joy and renewal. The living room, once quiet and subdued, now bore all the signs of a celebration. Balloons hung cheerfully from the corners, streamers danced lightly in the breeze from the open windows, and a delicious aroma wafted from the kitchen. Gerald and Clara had pulled out all the stops to make this homecoming one to remember, their hearts brimming with anticipation.

"They're here!" Gerald called out, his voice carrying through the house as he caught sight of Vihan's car pulling into the driveway. His excitement was infectious, and Clara hurried to the front door, her face lighting up with a mixture of joy and relief.

The car door opened, and out spilled Roselle and Liana, their faces glowing with happiness. They looked up at the house, their eyes wide with wonder at the decorations and the warmth that seemed to radiate from every corner. Veronica stepped out next, holding Vihan's hand, a quiet but visible unity between them that hadn't been there before.

Clara rushed forward, her arms wide open. "Oh, my little angels!" she exclaimed, pulling both girls into a tight hug. Roselle giggled, and Liana squealed, the sound of their laughter filling the air.

Gerald joined them, his usual lighthearted smile stretching ear to ear as he patted Vihan on the shoulder. “Welcome back, my boy,” he said warmly.

Inside, the atmosphere was nothing short of jubilant. The girls immediately dove into the colorful chaos of the living room. Liana dragged Roselle toward her toy chest, her voice bubbling with excitement. “Look at this one, Roselle! And this! It’s my favorite!” she said, pulling out dolls, puzzles, and stuffed animals faster than Roselle could process. Roselle, captivated by her sister’s enthusiasm, sat on the carpet, engrossed in the miniature tea party Liana had set up. Their laughter mingled, a harmonious melody of newfound sisterhood.

Meanwhile, in the kitchen, Clara set out plates of cookies and glasses of lemonade, her heart full as she watched the girls play. “It’s been so long since this house felt alive,” she whispered to Gerald, who nodded, his usual playful demeanor softening into something more tender.

Vihan stood nearby, watching the scene with a mixture of gratitude and regret. Gathering his courage, he turned to Gerald and Clara, his voice steady but filled with emotion. “I owe you both an apology,” he began. “For everything. For the way I left, for the pain I caused Veronica, and for all the time Roselle had to spend away from this warmth, this love.”

Clara stepped forward, her eyes kind. “What’s important is that you’re here now, Vihan. You’ve made things right. That’s what matters.”

Gerald, ever the wise and lighthearted soul, clapped a hand on Vihan’s shoulder. “Listen, son,” he said with a grin, “life’s not about getting everything right the first time.

It's about fixing what you've messed up and moving forward. And from what I see here, you're doing just that. Just remember—love and family? They're worth every bit of effort."

Vihan nodded, his throat tight with emotion. He embraced both Gerald and Clara, feeling a deep sense of belonging he hadn't felt in years.

The evening unfolded with pure joy. The girls' laughter echoed through the house as they chased each other around the living room. Veronica watched them with tears in her eyes, her heart overflowing with gratitude. Vihan joined in their play, lifting Liana onto his shoulders as Roselle tried to "catch" her. Clara and Gerald looked on, their faces glowing with pride and contentment.

As the night wore on, the family gathered around the table, sharing stories, laughter, and promises for the future. It wasn't just a meal—it was a celebration of unity, a testament to the strength of love and the power of forgiveness.

For the first time in what felt like forever, the house was filled with joy, hope, and the beautiful chaos of family life. The past was behind them, and ahead lay a future brimming with possibilities—a future they would face together, hand in hand, as a family.

Final Thoughts: A Letter to readers on Love and Marriage

Dear Readers,

As you close this book, I want to speak to you, not as an author, but as someone who has seen how love can both break and heal. Through Veronica and Vihan's story, I've tried to capture something we all know but often forget - that beneath our everyday moments lie countless chances to mend what's broken.

You see, love isn't just about the big moments. It's in the morning coffee you make together, the unsaid 'I love you' in a packed lunch, the gentle touch when passing in the hallway. But sometimes, we let these small moments slip away. We get busy. We get tired. We forget to look into each other's eyes.

To the husbands reading this: Remember when you first fell in love? How you noticed everything about her? Maybe lately, you've been so focused on providing the best life that you've forgotten to provide your presence. It's easy to think that working late shows love. But sometimes, just sitting quietly with her, hearing about her day, means more than any paycheck could.

To the wives: Your silence doesn't protect love - it slowly smothers it. Like Veronica, you might think keeping the peace keeps the love. But your feelings matter. Your dreams matter. Your voice matters. Love shouldn't feel like holding your breath.

To both partners: Take a moment. Right now. Think about the last time you really talked - not about bills or children or chores, but about hopes, fears, dreams. When did you last hold hands just because? When did you last say "I'm sorry" and really mean it?

Marriage isn't about being perfect. It's about being present. About choosing, every day, to turn towards each other instead of away. About seeing your partner's flaws and loving them anyway. About letting your own guards down and trusting that love will catch you.

Remember, every couple you see that's grown old together didn't get there by accident. They got there by choosing each other, again and again, especially when it was hard. Especially when it hurt. Especially when it would have been easier to walk away.

Love isn't just a feeling that stays by itself. It's like a garden - it needs tending. It needs water. It needs care. Sometimes it needs pruning. But mostly, it needs two people who never stop believing in its growth.

Let this story be more than just words on paper. Let it be the gentle nudge you needed to turn to each other tonight and say what's in your heart. Because love, real love, begins in these moments of courage.

With hope and faith in your love,

Nadeera Goonetilleke

THE END

www.ingramcontent.com/pod-product-compliance
Lightning Source LLC
LaVergne TN
LVHW010119170826
845678LV00012B/2498
9798230829256